This book belongs to

....

Also by Matt Beighton

Poetry

Tig You're It: And other poems from the playground

The Shadowland Chronicles

The Spyglass and the Cherry Tree
The Shadowed Eye

Monstacademy Series

The Halloween Parade
The Egyptian Treasure
The Grand High Monster
The Machu Picchu Mystery
The Magic Knight

For Younger Readers

Spot The Dot

For Phoebe and Willow

MONSTACADEMY
THE EGYPTIAN TREASURE

Printed in the United Kingdom
First Printing, 2018

A CIP catalogue record for this book is available from the British Library.

ISBN (Standard Edition): 978-1-9997244-4-3
ISBN (Dyslexia Friendly): 978-1-9997244-7-4

www.mattbeighton.co.uk
www.monstacademy.com

The Egyptian Treasure

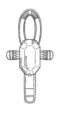

CHAPTER 1

A New Teacher

The wind was bitterly cold and the threat of snow was still very much on the cards as Trixie Grimble trudged back up the stone steps of Monstacademy on a foggy February morning. Despite the wretched weather, she couldn't wait to meet up with her friends once again. Gloria and Colin, a vegetarian vampire and a cursed werepoodle who she had befriended before Christmas, had both written to her over the holidays, but she was eager to talk to them properly.

Most of the holidays had been spent trying to find things to do outside of the house. When she had first moved out of her bedroom to start at

Monstacademy, Trixie's mother had turned it into a training room for her kitten circus. Trixie had been dismayed to find her mother had moved all of her furniture down to the shed at the bottom of the garden.

Sheds are cold and damp places at the best of times, but in the middle of a very cold and very wet English winter, they are practically unbearable. After the first night of nearly freezing to death, Trixie had stolen every blanket in the house along with all of the coats and jumpers for good measure. She'd used these to make a giant woolly cocoon and had still only just survived. Eventually, her mother had seen sense and allowed her back into the house but it had been touch-and-go for a while.

All of that didn't matter now that she was back at school. Trixie had never been so happy for a school holiday to end as she had this time. She was on the school Snaffleball team and couldn't wait for her first match; her nemesis Heston Gobswaddle had been expelled and, with any luck, Esme Furfang, the werewolf she had so thoroughly embarrassed entirely by accident, would have come down with a serious case of wolf-lice and taken the rest of the year off.

Trixie's mother had left her at the end of the long gravel path that led to the school, and Trixie was soon greeted at the large wooden doors by Grimsby, the school's janitor.

Grimsby wasn't so much a traditional monster as he was a monstrous thing pieced together from the parts of lots of different people. He often had to stitch himself together when the more mean-spirited students laid traps for him, and he looked like a human patchwork quilt.

The small monster took Trixie's case from her and welcomed her with a lopsided smile. He appeared to have made an effort for the new term and was dressed in an ill-fitting and pieced-together tuxedo that he had topped off with a lopsided top hat. He clearly hadn't been able to find a suitable feather to place in the brim, and so he'd glued a dead seagull on top.

Trixie had to stifle a giggle at the overall effect.

"Your friends are already here, miss," he lisped. Grimsby always lisped. It was the extra teeth that he'd had fitted after a terrible magical accident involving a hungry octopus. "They are waiting for you in your room."

Not even stopping to thank him, Trixie leapt past Grimsby and shot up the spiralling stone stairs that led to their dormitories. Colin and Gloria were lounging around messing up Trixie's bed when she burst through the door. They leapt up to give her a warm hug.

"It's so good to be back!" Trixie exclaimed when she'd finally managed to break away from her friends.

"Well, there's exciting news already!" said Gloria in a hushed but frantic whisper. "There's a new teacher, Mr Hairsnit, who I just know I'm going to get along with so well!"

Behind her, Colin made a swooning gesture. "Oh, Mr Hairsnit, you are *so* handsome!"

"Oh, cut it out!" Gloria had gone bright red about her cheeks and gave Colin a hard punch on his arm. "I just mean that he is a very well-respected werewolf back home and we are lucky to have him here to teach us. He's quite an adventurer, apparently."

"That's not the only news, either." interrupted Colin. "Heston is back."

Heston Gobswaddle had very nearly caused Monstacademy to close down before Christmas when he'd conjured up a devious plan to shrink all of the people of Wexbridge. Luckily, Trixie, Colin and Gloria had managed to stop him at the last minute. Trixie was dismayed to hear that he was back. Unlike Miss Brimstone who seemed to have a soft spot for the ugly wizard, Miss Flopsbottom had seemed as eager to see him gone as the rest of them had. The large, friendly vampire and current headmistress of Monstacademy had been very impressed with Trixie and her friends when they'd managed to foil his plan.

"He's done all of his community service, so they've allowed him back. He's not learnt, though. He's brought a pet with him!"

"A pet?" asked Trixie, shocked. "I didn't think we were allowed pets."

"We're not!" Gloria huffed. "He's done it anyway. It just shows that he'll never learn."

"What has he brought?"

"A grey rat. A filthy, hairy, germy rat." Gloria folded her arms in despair.

"Oh. I thought it'd be something more exciting." Trixie was disappointed at the news.

"Well, how was your Christmas anyway?" asked Colin.

"Cold! I had to sleep in the garden shed!"

"I have to sleep in a dog basket on the porch," laughed Colin.

"And I have to sleep in a windy castle in the middle of nowhere," pointed out Gloria.

"Yes, well, you're used to it. I'm used to a nice, warm bedroom. When I got home, my bedroom was full of circus equipment and cats. There was a tiny trapeze hung across the ceiling, and my bed had been replaced with a ring of fire. Plus, it smelled of cat wee!"

The three of them fell about laughing at her mother's plans for her cat circus. "It was all right in the end, though. She let me back into the house for Christmas Day. It was a regular Christmas miracle! At least I was in my own bed for my birthday."

"Oh, I'm so sorry!" Gloria was even more pale than usual with embarrassment. "I didn't know. How old were you?"

"Ten. It's all right. I didn't tell anyone. I'm not

that bothered."

"Ten?" Colin laughed. "You can tell you're not a monster! Me and Gloria are both much nearer to a hundred years old. We live a long time." Trixie smiled at her friends and gave them both a big hug. It was such a relief to be back.

Eventually, they had to get dressed and make their way to the main hall for dinner. As always, they sat on their own in a corner trying to avoid everyone else. Heston made a particular point of glaring at them throughout his meal and, annoyingly, so did Esme Furfang. Trixie was sure that Esme was even more annoyed at her because she had been picked to play on the school Snaffleball team and Esme hadn't. Whatever it was, it would have to wait. Once again, disaster wasn't far away.

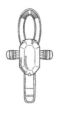

CHAPTER 2

Queen Ankhesenamun

The first lesson of the term was history and was being taught by Mr Hairsnit. He wasn't what Trixie had imagined. From Gloria's description, she'd imagined a young pop star, but he wasn't like that at all.

For a start, he was older than she'd expected with short silver hair that he wore under a wide leather hat and that blended into a bushy grey beard. The beard covered his mouth and must have surely tickled his nose. His nose was rather large and pointed off to one side and his ears were very pointy, as though they'd forgotten to change back from his wolf form.

He had an old, stained, brown leather jacket

with patches of tartan material sewed over the elbows and spoke with a soft but firm voice.

Gloria was over the moon. She had made sure to bring all of her very best stationery along to impress him. Her pencil practically sparkled. Colin found the whole thing hilarious and was desperately trying his hardest not to giggle. Gloria was more annoyed about the fact that Heston had brought his pet rat into the classroom.

"Look at him with the little grey beast on his shoulder. It's disgusting!" she whispered to Trixie as they waited for the rest of the class to arrive. "I bet it's shedding hairs all over the classroom. It's unhygienic, you know!"

"Miss Toothsome!" They hadn't noticed Mr Hairsnit wandering around the classroom and popping up behind them. He'd caught Gloria off guard, and she quickly turned as red as a strawberry. "If you have a problem with Mr Gobswaddle's pet, perhaps you should take it up with Miss Flopsbottom instead of wasting my time. How about you, Miss Grimble? Would you like to blame poor Miss Furfang for your noisy behaviour, or did you embarrass her enough last term? Now, if you don't mind, I'd like to start the lesson."

Trixie turned bright red. She hated having a reputation. Gloria's embarrassment turned to anger as Heston turned towards her and stuck out his tongue. His pet rat, seeing what its owner was doing, turned and stuck out its tongue as well.

Gloria was just about to get up and say something rather mean when Mr Hairsnit took his place at the front of the class and started the lesson. Trixie patted her friend on the shoulder and tried unsuccessfully to calm her down. Esme took this opportunity to throw a balled-up piece of paper at Trixie's head.

As a special treat, Mr Hairsnit had invited an Ancient Egyptian mummy to come in and talk to them about what it used to be like for monsters. If, like me, you think Mummies are all bandages and funny walks, then you would be wrong. Even though she looked old and worn, the mummy dazzled. She was wearing a lot of colourful make-up and was dripping with gems and gold. There were no bandages at all.

"She's beautiful!" whispered Trixie to her friends.

"I'll say!" laughed Colin before Gloria gave him a sharp elbow to the ribs. She wasn't in the mood for silliness.

"Children," introduced Mr Hairsnit, "this is Queen Ankhesenamun. She was a ruler of the Ancient Egyptians and wife of Tutankhamen. She has come here today to talk to you about ancient magic and what life was like for monsters back then. Make sure to take notes. There will be homework."

With a flourish of his hands and an over-the-top bow, Mr Hairsnit stepped aside and allowed the queen to step to the front of the class. Her voice was dry like the sands of her homeland and came out in a whisper. She explained all about her people and how everything they did was to please their gods. Trixie got the impression that the gods were very important to Ancient Egyptians.

Eventually the subject of magic came up, and Trixie was worried to notice Heston suddenly sit up straight and take an interest in the lesson. She poked Gloria and pointed him out. Gloria frowned but said nothing.

At the front of the class, Queen Ankhesenamun was taking a piece of jewellery out of an old cloth bag. "This is perhaps the most magical item in all of Ancient Egypt," she whispered breathlessly. "This is the Ankhstone. It once belonged to Heka, the Egyptian god of magic. Legend says that many thousands of years ago, Heka dropped it whilst travelling across the skies. It fell to Earth and was picked up by one of my ancestors. Over time, it was passed down through the generations until it was handed to my great-grandmother. She gave it to my mother and then to me.

"Unfortunately, when I died, it was buried with me deep beneath the stones of my pyramid, and so it wasn't seen again for thousands of years. Until one day, I woke up and felt like going for a walk." As the queen spoke, the children all leaned forwards in their chairs for a better look. Even Mr Hairsnit was perched precariously on the edge of his seat.

The gemstone was a vivid turquoise and the size of a fist. Even in the dull light of the classroom, it sparkled brightly and cast blue-green flashes against the walls whenever it moved. It was set into the centre of a solid gold ankh that was only a little bigger than the stone itself. It was very beautiful.

"What does it do?" asked Heston, a little too eagerly for Trixie's comfort.

"The power of the stone comes from our gods and gives whoever holds it the power to control other people. They can control their minds, their thoughts and their wishes. It is a very powerful weapon if it is not used carefully. Luckily, there is a magic spell that you need to say to make it work." The queen finished with a smile and chuckle. "And

I'll never tell any of you what it is."

Trixie was annoyed to see Heston give the queen a big round of applause before he was shushed into quiet by Mr Hairsnit.

"Back when I was alive, we would use this to control the people of Egypt. There were many more monsters then, and they lived amongst the humans. Did you know that Tutankhamen was a werewolf? Not many people do."

"Now Queen Ankhesenamun has been very generous indeed, children. She has agreed to let us keep the Ankhstone on display in the library for the whole term so that we can all study it in greater detail. Isn't that kind of her?" asked Mr Hairsnit.

They all agreed that it was indeed very kind, and Heston led them in yet another round of applause for the queen.

Once all of the questions had been asked and Heston had once again made his appreciation clear, Queen Ankhesenamun was escorted out of the class by Mr Hairsnit who dismissed the children with a disinterested wave of his hand. He was far too eager to keep the queen happy and barely paid them any notice as they filed out and made their way to their Latin lesson with Miss Brimstone. As punishment for her embarrassing behaviour at the Halloween Parade, Trixie still had to sit on her own facing the wall. It was boring.

Unfortunately, Latin wasn't any more interesting for Heston Gobswaddle, and so Trixie and the rest of her class had to put up with him constantly moaning and disrupting the lesson by firing spitballs at them all. Eventually, Miss Brimstone had had quite enough of him and sent him away to spend the rest of the day in detention with Miss Flopsbottom.

Later that evening, as they were all sitting down for dinner, a cacophony of sound erupted from the far end of the main hall. Several of the teachers burst in through the far doors and hurried over to Miss Brimstone whose face turned to stone. Even from the other side of the hall, Trixie could hear the banshee's loud, angry wail. Whatever she had been told, it wasn't good news. When she had composed herself, she scanned the room furiously as though looking hard for something she'd misplaced. Trixie found herself doing the same and wasn't surprised when she saw Heston's ugly sidekicks, Kevin Thimblenose who had a pumpkin for a head and a ghost called Dilbert Trompton who very much resembled a gorilla, sat next to an empty chair. Heston was nowhere to be seen. Trixie felt sure that whatever was happening had something to do with him.

It didn't take long before the whispers started to filter towards the back of the hall where Trixie, Colin and Gloria were sat. By the time the murmurs reached them, it had left in its wake a wave of panic and confusion.

"*It's been stolen! The Ankhstone, it's gone!*"

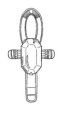

CHAPTER 3

Thief!

A s soon as it was confirmed that the Ankhstone had been stolen, the children were sent straight to their rooms to wait for further information. The whole school was abuzz with excitement. Nothing like this ever happened at Monstacademy. Can you imagine how much shock and excitement there would be at your school if the Queen – the real Queen of England that is – brought her Crown Jewels in to show you all and they were stolen? Now you can imagine a little bit of what the next few hours were like at Monstacademy.

It took a while, but by midnight the teachers had worked their way through all of the children in the school and questioned them all about where they had been. Since most of them had been in the hall eating dinner, it had seemed a very pointless exercise, but they did it nevertheless. Queen Ankhesenamun had been informed and was apparently very worried. Without the magic words, she was convinced that they didn't need to worry about somebody suddenly taking control of the minds of everyone at Monstacademy.

Colin wasn't so convinced, though. "Heston is behind this. We all know it!" he'd announced when Miss Brimstone had arrived to check that everyone was safely back in their rooms and that the missing Ankhstone wasn't being hidden by a student.

"Mr Curlyton, we do not blame people for crimes until they are proved guilty. Is that clear?"

"But –"

"But me no buts, mister. Do not argue, otherwise you will find yourself in detention. Is that clear? And what are you even doing in here? This is the girls' bedroom. You should be in your own!" Colin didn't bother to reply. He just sulked and moved over to Trixie's bed whilst the search continued.

Once Miss Brimstone had convinced herself that Trixie and her friends weren't behind the jewellery heist and had moved on to the next room with a disgruntled Colin in tow, Trixie turned to Gloria and laid out a plan.

"We know it's Heston. It has to be. We've just got to prove it. We should sneak down to the library tonight to see where the jewel was being kept to see if there are any clues? What do you think?"

"I think I want that little bogey to pay for this morning. Did you see him? Even his stinking rat stuck its tongue out at me! I swear the thing is cleverer than its owner."

"We probably need to get Colin to keep watch."

"Not after last time!" Gloria chuckled. The last time that Colin had kept watch he had got bored and stopped watching and one of Heston's friends had caught them sneaking around in his bedroom. "One of us can keep watch this time. We're more likely to stay awake!"

"Okay, but how will we get a message to him? Miss Brimstone won't let us into his room after kicking him out."

"Well, the boys' tower is opposite ours." At Monstacademy, there were several tall stone towers that surrounded the inner courtyard. Some of them were home to classrooms or the teachers' offices, but two of them contained the dormitories of the boys and girls. "It's not too far away. If you can keep an eye out for anyone below us, I have an idea."

"What are you going to do? We don't want to be spotted." Trixie was starting to get worried. Whatever Gloria had in mind, it sounded risky.

"Just keep an eye out. And meet us in the library in ten minutes." Gloria took off her dressing gown and started to stretch as though she were about to run a race. "Oh, and look away please."

Trixie did as she was told and turned to look at the bedroom door. She heard a soft pop and then a flapping sound. When she turned back round, Gloria had disappeared. Instead, there was a small black bat banging its head repeatedly against the window pane.

You might imagine that Trixie would be shocked by seeing her best friend turn into a bat. After all, she hadn't seen this trick before. It just goes to show just how Trixie had grown accustomed to Monstacademy that she just giggled to herself and opened the window to let her friend out. She kept an eye on the courtyard below, but there was nobody about at this hour.

Once Gloria had made it safely across to the boys' tower, Trixie tiptoed out of the bedroom and made her way quietly down to the library. Luckily, she was barefoot otherwise her shoes would have made quite the noise on the giant flagstones that covered the floor.

Once she'd made it to the library, Trixie found the empty glass cabinet that had been used to hold the Ankhstone and crouched down behind it to wait for her friends.

It took a lot longer than ten minutes before Gloria and Colin finally wandered into the library arguing amongst themselves in hushed whispers.

"I told you not to go rushing out of the room like that," chastised Gloria. "You very nearly got caught!"

"Yes, but I didn't, did I?" Colin was clearly feeling very put upon by Gloria's moaning and tried to turn the conversation towards the missing jewel, with no success.

"He went barging straight out of his bedroom and very nearly bumped into Mr Hairsnit. We'd have been busted for sure if I hadn't dragged him quickly around the corner." Trixie listened as Gloria laid out just how clumsy Colin had been.

"What was Mr Hairsnit doing out and about this late anyway? That's what I want to know," argued Colin.

Gloria, as ever, leapt to the teacher's defence. "Well, he quite obviously just wants to make sure that everything is safe around the school and nothing else gets stolen. Who knows what the Ankhstone might do in the wrong hands?"

"Hmf." Colin snorted and tried to move away.

"Guys, over there! What's that?" Trixie raced over to a grate in the wall. It looked just like every other grate on the wall. "The grey hairs! They're trapped in the metal at the side. This is how the thief must have got in and out. They must have caught themselves and left this behind."

The trio bent down for a closer look. Sure enough, there were a dozen or so short, thin, grey hairs wedged into the grill.

"I know where they're from!" exclaimed Colin as

he stood up. "Who do we know who has a small, grey furry friend?"

"Heston?" Trixie wasn't sure. "But how could a rat steal the Ankhstone?"

"He trained it to stick its tongue out at me. I bet he could definitely train it to steal something for him." Gloria was so excited that she was forgetting to whisper. "I knew it was that toad! Let's go and tell Miss Flopsbottom."

"She'll be asleep. I don't want to wake her." Trixie had another idea. "You said Mr Hairsnit was still awake, though. We could go and find him and tell him."

"But Gloria doesn't have her best dress on," laughed Colin as they quietly left the library and made their way back towards the boys' dormitory.

"Oh, do shut up, Colin," hissed Gloria as she thumped him on the arm yet again.

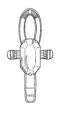

CHAPTER 4

An Angry Ferret

Trixie and her friends tiptoed through the empty corridors of Monstacademy. Mr Hairsnit hadn't been in the corridors outside of the boys' dormitories, and so they had set off again for the tower that contained the teachers' offices hoping to find him there. Even barefoot, their steps seemed to echo in the silent hallways and more than once Gloria had to hiss for them to quiet. The fact that they only had specks of moonlight to see by didn't help and made the whole thing much scarier than they would have liked.

In fact, it was so tense that when a soft voice came out of the darkness behind them and commanded,

"What are you three doing out of bed at this late hour?"

Gloria screamed out loud, spun on her heels and kicked Mr Hairsnit right between the legs! He doubled over with a heavy sigh and collapsed in a heap. When the teacher had finally recovered himself and Gloria had exhausted herself apologising, he lit a candle and at last they were able to see each other clearly.

"Well, moving on," he winced with a growl, "I ask you again. What are you doing out of bed at this hour?"

"I'm really so very sorry—" Gloria continued to apologise through streams of tears, but Colin quickly cut her off.

"We were looking for you, sir. We know who stole the Ankhstone."

A strange look passed over the werewolf's face. He looked almost confused or worried. "I beg your pardon?"

"We've been investigating, and we found some short grey hairs in the grate next to the cabinet where the Ankhstone was held." Trixie was very pleased with her discovery and wanted to be the one to tell the teacher. "Heston has brought his pet rat to school with him and he has grey hair. He got his rat to steal it for him!"

Mr Hairsnit sighed and put his arms around the three children. "I want you to listen to me, okay? I don't know who stole the jewel, but I very much doubt it was a rat. This is a problem for the teachers to investigate. Do you understand? I want you three to have nothing more to do with it. That is an order.

"Now, correct me if I'm wrong, Miss Grimble, but don't you have a Snaffleball match in the morning?"

In all of the excitement and mystery, Trixie had completely forgotten that her very first Snaffleball match for Monstacademy was first thing in the morning. It was already past midnight!

The three children quickly made their apologies before rushing off back to their beds. Behind them, Trixie half-heard their teacher having a hurried and whispered conversation, but she had no time to concentrate on that now. She was desperately in need of some rest.

Once she was in bed, Trixie tried her hardest to get to sleep, but the sun was starting to leak in through the bedroom window before she finally managed to drift off. It didn't feel like she had even closed her eyes before the cockerel in the courtyard crowed his alarm and Trixie dragged herself from her bed. She was furious for allowing herself to get dragged along with the adventure last night when she should have been in bed resting. You know just how hard it is to think or run around when you haven't had enough sleep. Imagine how Trixie felt knowing that she had to go out and play a game of Snaffleball in front of all of the teachers and other children.

As always there was a large breakfast prepared in the main hall, but Trixie wasn't hungry. She just sat with her eyes closed and her head resting on the wall whilst Colin wolfed down bacon and sausage and Gloria had a bowl of parsnip porridge.

When the time came to make their way down to the pitch by the big pond, Trixie was no less tired. She made her way into the changing rooms with the rest of her team and put on her uniform.

The Snaffleball players all wore dark red T-shirts with gold shorts. Trixie's top was two sizes too big and swamped her. She had to tie an old piece of string around the shorts to keep them from falling down. Before they made their way to the pitch, their Snaffleball coach, Mr Fetch, gave them some last-minute instructions and some tips about what Cromley's, their opponent, were good at. Trixie didn't pay any attention, though. Her mind was completely blank as she stepped out onto the large pitch.

On one side, the Cromley fans were stood shivering in the cold weather. The net across the court was shaking in the strong breeze that blew up towards the castle. Opposite them, the Monstacademy supporters were slightly better protected by a small wooden hut fitted out with benches.

There weren't many supporters on either side, and Trixie was relieved to see that Heston had stayed away. She was dismayed to see Esme Furfang glaring at her, half-hidden by several other spectators on the sidelines, but even as she tried to match her stare, the werewolf turned and stormed away. Miss Flopsbottom was there in her thick purple coat along with Miss Brimstone and Mr Hairsnit. Trixie couldn't afford to embarrass herself today.

Trixie was the Snaffler for Monstacademy which meant that she had the job of moving around inside the Cromley half of the court trying to catch the ball and to put it into the wooden bucket that stood on the back line. If her opponents had the ball, she had to try to snaffle it from them.

Normally, she was very good at this and would spend the duration of the game running backwards and forwards shouting for the ball. Today, she was so tired that she was struggling to run from one side to the other and missed several good chances to score by dropping the ball.

Then, she saw her chance. There were only a few minutes left and the game was tied when Trixie's teammate Gladys (the poor girl who turned into a cat every third Thursday) hit the ball clean over the net straight into her hands.

Trixie managed to catch it and turned around towards the bucket. There it was, right in front of her. She couldn't miss. Without even taking time to think, Trixie pulled her arm back ready to throw the ball, only it wasn't a ball anymore.

Somehow the ball had disappeared and been replaced by an angry ferret. It took one look at

Trixie before biting her hard on the nose and scampering off down her arm and under her jumper. Panicking, she ripped her uniform off and threw it and the ferret into the long grass. She stood forlornly on the pitch in nothing but her vest and pants as the audience erupted into laughter.

Out of the corner of her eye, Trixie saw the ball roll slowly away. She turned to appeal to the referee only to see him on his hands and knees trying to find his glasses which had been conveniently knocked from his head.

The Cromley fans cheered, and the Monstacademy fans booed. Trixie was mortified. She looked over and saw the hurt in Miss Flopsbottom's eyes as though she'd done it on purpose. Miss Brimstone looked positively delighted. To her, it was just another reason to dislike Trixie.

The referee blew his whistle to put Trixie out her misery, even though there were still a few minutes of the match left. Trixie trudged off the pitch without shaking the hands of the other players and wandered over towards Colin and Gloria.

"I don't know what happened!" Trixie kept repeating herself in the hope that they would believe her. "I would have scored!"

"Of course, you would. You were doing so well until then." The voice seemed to come out of thin air. Trixie and her friends stood looking around trying to find where it had come from.

As they watched, the air shimmered slightly and then suddenly Esme Furfang was stood in front of them. She was spinning the match ball on her finger. "A pretty cool potion, don't you think?" the werewolf giggled to herself. "Who knew you could make an invisibility potion? It gave me just enough time to make sure that you got what was coming to you. Now you know how I felt!"

Esme ran away before Colin and Gloria could get hold of her. Trixie noticed that the werewolf looked up to the teachers as she left. She was almost certain that she saw her enemy nod her head slightly. Trixie wouldn't have been surprised if Miss Brimstone was behind this whole thing. It would be just her style. She had bigger things to worry about for now, though.

"Leave her. We've got other problems. I've not given up on proving that Heston stole the Ankhstone. If he did, it's because he wants to use it," Trixie said to her friends as she trudged through the wet mud back towards the castle. "And we saw last time that he has some pretty horrible ideas."

CHAPTER 5

Unfair Punishment

The very next day was a Saturday, and Trixie decided to confront Heston about the great Ankhstone theft. She was absolutely sure that he was behind it, and she wanted to see if he would confess.

But first she wanted to see if she could find any more evidence. Gloria and Colin were already in the library working on their homework when she wandered in just after lunch. There was no noise other than the sound of children reading quietly and scribbling notes down in their books.

Mr Hairsnit had set them the task of researching Ancient Egyptian monsters, and Gloria had thrown herself into her work head first. She'd been

45

spending every day in the library reading every book that she could get her hands on. She was still desperately trying to please their new teacher. Colin had tagged along because Gloria didn't notice when he copied her notes. Trixie didn't bother to disturb her friends. She wanted to be able to skulk around on her own.

There was a ring of rope around the glass case that had held the Ankhstone. Trixie ducked under it and started to look in the shadows. There weren't many people in this area of the library, and so she was able to move about without being detected, so long as she wasn't too noisy. She was disappointed that there were no more clues near the case. But when she started to look behind the plant pots and statues that stood against the wall, she spotted something that caused her to stop in her tracks.

Being careful not to attract any attention, Trixie raced over to her friends and dragged them back to the dark corner of the library.

"There!" She was pointing at a statue of an elderly vampire smoking a pipe.

"It's a statue." said Gloria matter-of-factly.

"Look behind it!" Trixie was practically bouncing with excitement and pushed the others forward so that they could get a better look.

"A banana skin?" Colin looked very confused. "You dragged us here for a banana skin?"

"Dilbert! He loves bananas. He's practically a gorilla. He must have been here with Heston when he stole the Ankhstone. Then he gave it to his rat who escaped through the grating. It all makes sense!" Trixie was practically shouting. Gloria dragged her back out of the roped off area and into the corridor. The librarian was a Gargoyle and was known to stick noisy children onto the roof of the tower until they learnt their lesson.

"Look, I want Heston to pay for what he's done as much as you, but you can't keep running around waving a banana like it's some sort of weapon."

"We know it was him." Trixie was getting very annoyed at Gloria. Why couldn't she see how obvious it was? "He's over there. I'm going to tell him we know it was him." Before Gloria could stop her, Trixie stomped across the hallway and stood staring at Heston and his cronies. They were picking their noses and comparing who had the biggest bogey. Trixie barged in front of Dilbert Trompton and Kevin Thimblenose who started flicking theirs at each other and looked Heston straight in the eyes.

"We know you did it," she said triumphantly. "We know you stole the Ankhstone."

"Huh?" He looked very confused.

"We found the grey hairs on the grating where your rat got stuck trying to escape with the jewel, and we found the banana skin behind the statue. That was Dilbert's." Trixie folded her arms and waited to see what Heston would do next.

"You think I stole the Ankhstone?"

"Yes."

"And then my rat ran away with it?"

"Er, yes."

"And Dilbert left behind a banana?"

"The skin, yes." Now that Heston was saying it out loud, Trixie was starting to regret confronting him. It really wasn't very much evidence to go on.

"Okay. Ignoring the fact that my rat is suffering from a cold and can barely get out of his bed, let alone carry a heavy piece of jewellery, I wasn't even here when the Ankhstone was stolen. I was in detention with Miss Flopsbottom. I was there all evening."

Trixie suddenly felt very embarrassed. She remembered now that Heston and the head teacher hadn't been at the meal in the main hall the night the Ankhstone was stolen. Miss Flopsbottom would be able to tell her for sure, but she knew that even Heston wouldn't lie about something so obvious.

"I guess that super-amazing detective skills aren't your special power after all." Heston and his friends were enjoying themselves. "Once again, Trixie, you prove that you really are the *worst* monster in school!"

"Trixie Grimble!" the loud voice of Miss Flopsbottom, the headmistress, echoed down the corridor. Heston and his friends ran in the opposite direction. "Trixie Grimble!" Miss Flopsbottom rounded the corner with Esme Furfang leading the way.

"There she is!" growled the werewolf. "She did it!"

Miss Flopsbottom didn't waste any time, grabbing Trixie by her shoulder and dragging her away.

"You will come with me right now, young lady!" she thundered.

"What have I done, Miss Flopsbottom?" asked Trixie. As far as she was aware, she hadn't done anything wrong lately. It had been something of a good streak for her.

"If you don't know, missy, I'm not about to tell you. But suffice to say that Miss Furfang is extremely upset."

Trixie really tried her hardest to think about what this might all be about. There was nothing, though. There was no way that Miss Flopsbottom could know that she had just confronted Heston about the theft of the stone, and *surely* she didn't think that Trixie was behind *that*. Whatever stunt

Esme was pulling was certainly working.

After a long but very brisk walk through the school grounds, during which every pupil stopped to stare, Trixie was plopped down in a hard wooden chair in front of Miss Flopsbottom's desk. A sheet of paper was shuffled in front of her, and a pencil dropped into her lap.

"Please, Miss Flopsbottom. I don't understand-"

"I do not need you to understand, girl. I just need you to do as you are told. You will write out what you did and why you must never do it again. Is that clear?"

"But—"

"A thousand times! Now get to it!"

Trixie looked up in despair at the headmistress. This was completely unlike her. Even when Trixie had been in trouble, and that had been often when she first started at Monstacademy, Miss Flopsbottom had never been anything but compassionate and understanding. Now she was just being cruel. Trixie caught her eyes as she tried to look away. There was something wrong. Her eyes were wide open and staring into the distance. She didn't blink, either. Something wasn't quite right, but Trixie couldn't place her finger on it.

She had little chance to dwell on the matter as Miss Flopsbottom barged out of the room leaving Trixie on her own.

Taking a chance, Trixie scribbled a quick message onto the paper explaining that she really didn't know what she had done wrong and then left quietly and headed back to her bedroom.

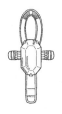

CHAPTER 6

An Upside-Down Potion

"I told you not to go and talk to him." It was later that day, and Gloria was pacing backwards and forwards wearing a hole in their bedroom carpet. "Now he knows that we're on to him."

"Well, it doesn't matter anyway," barked Colin. The moon was going to full that evening, and he was looking more and more poodle-like as it drew closer. Even though he still looked like a boy, albeit an incredibly hairy one, he was lounging in his furry dog basket and chewing on his pink bone. It squeaked constantly. "He told you he wasn't even there when it was stolen."

"He wouldn't need to be, would he?" Trixie still

wasn't giving up. "He could've sent his rat to do all of the work with Dilbert or Kevin. They could've stolen it whilst he was safely doing his detention."

"Give it up, Trix." Colin tried to scratch behind his ear with his foot. It would be a few more hours before he'd be able to. "He's innocent. I don't like it either, but it looks like this is one thing that Heston didn't do."

"What about Esme Furfang?" Trixie was still reeling from whatever it was that the werewolf had accused her of doing. "She's been acting particularly evil lately, even for her."

"I doubt it. She's too much of a teacher's pet," Gloria said. The other two looked at each other with a smirk.

"Yeah, *she's* the teacher's pet," Colin said, mainly to Trixie.

"Then who *did* steal it, clever clogs?"

"Who knows?" Colin shrugged. "Maybe Mr Hairsnit?"

"As if!" Gloria threw a cushion at Colin. He caught it in his teeth and growled. "He's a renowned adventurer who has found treasure all over the world. I was reading about him for our homework. I had no idea how old he is. He looks so young."

Colin and Trixie rolled their eyes at each other but said nothing. Gloria continued, "He was alive during the time of the Ancient Egyptians. Here, look in this book." She handed over a thick, leather-bound encyclopaedia to Colin, who sagged under its weight. "I doubt he would steal something as ordinary as the Ankhstone."

"What about its magical power?" Colin pushed.

"I've been reading about that. Apparently, a lot of ancient artifacts were thought to have magical powers, but really they were just superstition. I don't know if it really *is* magical at all. Heka was just one of many gods, and we don't even know if they existed *at all*."

"You just don't want it to be Mr Hairsnit. Isn't it suspicious that he was alive back then and just happened to bring Queen Ankhesenamun to Monstacademy? What if he did it just so that he could steal the stone?" Colin had been flicking through the pages of the heavy book, and he suddenly slammed his finger down on one of the pages. "Look at this!"

Gloria and Trixie leaned in to have a better look at the dusty old page. It was marked with brown stains and the edges were torn slightly, but the writing was still clear. Colin read the paragraph that had caught his eye. "It says here that Mr Hairsnit was actually called Heka-Messes back then."

"That means Son of Heka." Gloria translated without thinking. "I've been looking into their names," she finished when her friends looked at her oddly.

Colin frowned at her and continued reading. "It also says that he was a vizier to Tutankhamen. That's like an adviser. So, if he was an adviser to King Tut, he'd know all about Queen Ankhesenamun and would have advised her as well. This is really suspicious, Gloria. Even you have to admit."

Gloria didn't say anything but snatched the book back from Colin.

"So if he did know them and his name means Son of Heka…" Trixie trailed off. She was thinking as she spoke and wasn't quite sure what it meant, but she felt sure that it meant *something*.

"Maybe he believes that the Ankhstone is rightfully his." Gloria almost whispered the words as though saying them might somehow make them true. "Maybe he did steal it after all."

"Exactly!" Colin looked incredibly smug that he had managed to solve the case. The others weren't fully convinced just yet.

"We need to know for sure before we say anything. We can't just barge up to him and accuse him of stealing the stone," Gloria warned. She glanced at Trixie who looked sheepishly at her shoes.

Colin threw his hands up dramatically but accepted Gloria's argument. "Fine then. What shall we do next?"

Gloria looked at her watch and started to get into a flap. "Next? We're late for our potions lesson with Mr Snickletinkle. You know how he gets."

They certainly did know how he got, and so the three of them threw their bags onto their backs and flew down the stairs to the basement beneath the tower where their potions lesson was just getting started. They barged through the door and flopped down at their desks as everyone turned to look at the noisy intrusion.

"Well, well, well. If it isn't Parsnip, Poodle and Pathetic!" Heston's joke got a raucous laugh from his friends and a stick of chalk thrown at his head from Mr Snickletinkle. Red-faced and out of breath, the trio took their seats and hoped that their tables would swallow them up whole.

Mr Snickletinkle was short for a vampire and very skinny, and so he stood on top of a stool whenever he spoke to the class. Apparently, he had placed the stool on an uneven flagstone that morning as it wobbled every time he spoke. Watching him try to keep his balance without taking his eyes off the class was like watching a giraffe try to stand on a beach ball.

"Today we have a very exciting lesson!" he began and had to rebalance himself. "It will be the Easter Fete before we know it, and it is traditional that the first-year pupils put together a display of fun and exciting potions. They really can be anything that you like. Within reason, of course!" He paused once again whilst he regained his balance. "In the past, we have had potions that turn the victim's hair pink and ones that make their mouths hang wide open for an hour or two. All in good fun, of course. I just know that you will do us proud this year. I will personally be testing them all at the end of the lesson, so make sure they work." This caused Mr Snickletinkle to laugh so hard that the stool gave way completely and he flew into the air. He landed flat on his back with his feet pointing towards the ceiling. "Off you go then!" he wheezed from the floor.

This really was a very exciting lesson. Imagine your teacher giving you a whole lesson to write *whatever* you want or to draw a picture of anything that pops into your head! That's just how Trixie and her friends felt at that moment. Trixie, who still wasn't as good at potions as the rest of the class, decided to keep it simple. Her potion would make whoever drank it as light as a feather. She hoped that they would float away up to the ceiling with the slightest of breezes. Colin knew immediately was his was going to do.

"Mine will make you give out the biggest, loudest burp you've ever heard. But it won't just be once. You'll be burping for an hour." Trixie had never seen him so happy. Gloria was very secretive about hers and wouldn't tell anybody what she was doing. In the end, Trixie gave up asking and just concentrated on her own.

By the time Mr Snickletinkle called the lesson to a close, the room was filled with a fantastic array of multicoloured smokes and enchanting smells. Trixie was very impressed with how brave

Mr Snickletinkle was. After all, would you want to try so many different potions all made by children who hadn't the foggiest what they were supposed to be doing? Anything could happen!

Luckily, most of the potions seemed to do what they were supposed to. Gladys's purple concoction caused Mr Snickletinkle's ears to turn into big, floppy rabbit's ears and earned her an excited round of applause from the teacher. Heston's gave the vampire a terrible case of juicy spots. Esme gave Trixie a horrible smirk as her giggling potion had the desired effect on the teacher, and he responded by awarding her an emphatic handshake.

Trixie was over the moon and gave the werewolf a smirk of her own when her potion worked like a charm and they had to fetch a ladder to drag Mr Snickletinkle back down from the ceiling. She was concerned when Gloria refused to present a potion to Mr Snickletinkle.

Instead, she told him that it had gone very badly wrong and that she was sorry but she wouldn't be able to give him anything to try. He seemed disappointed but moved on to the last potion.

Colin's experiment had produced a vivid blue syrup that bubbled slowly in the glass beaker.

"And what is this, Mr Curlyton?"

"It's a burping potion, sir. It will make you burp. A lot!"

Trixie heard Heston giggling in the background and tried to ignore him. She wasn't sure she trusted Colin to have mixed the potion correctly. He was almost as bad as she was.

Mr Snickletinkle took a long swig before wiping his chin clean. "Ah fantastic! You've used a classic mixture of ginger, bat vomit and cow's earwax? The ginger goes in first, of course. That's the key thing."

"Erm." Colin looked very worried all of a sudden. "What would happen if I put the ginger in last? And twice as much of it at that?"

Now it was Mr Snickletinkle's turn to look concerned. "Are you telling me, Colin Curlyton, that you mixed a wind potion…*upside down*?"

Nobody spoke. They didn't need to. The cross-eyed look on the old vampire's face told them all they needed to know. There was a rumble from his stomach, much as you might hear as the last bit of water leaves a bathtub or if you stand next to a very poorly cow. And then it happened. Colin had certainly got part of the potion right. There really was a huge amount of loud wind suddenly exploding from a mortified Mr Snickletinkle. Unfortunately, it wasn't coming from his mouth as expected!

The important thing to remember at this point is, not only was Mr Snickletinkle exploding a large volume of air from his bottom, he was still suffering the light-as-a-feather effect of Trixie's potion. Put those together, and he shot around the room like a half-inflated balloon that had been let go.

"Colin!" he shouted as he bounced from wall to wall. "See me in my office this evening please. You have some practising to do."

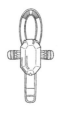

CHAPTER 7

An Important Discovery

When Colin sat down next to the girls in the library the next day, they were still laughing about the unfortunate mishap with his potion.

"Shut up, you guys. It's not that funny! Mr Snickletinkle made me mix the potion a dozen times last night so that I would get it right. He made me taste each one to make sure. I was still burping at four o'clock this morning."

This latest admission caused the girls to fall about laughing even more. They only quietened down when the librarian dragged herself over to their corner and demanded silence.

When at last they were quiet, Trixie asked the

question that was on everyone's mind. "What do we do about Mr Hairsnit now? We need to know what he is up to."

"I think I might have an idea." Gloria looked nervous. "We could follow him around and see what he gets up to."

"He'd see us," said Colin dismissively. "We'd never be able to get close enough to see or hear anything."

Gloria looked shiftily at the floor and pulled a bottle of deep red liquid from a pocket inside her robe.

"What is that?" Colin had had quite enough of potions for the time being. "Isn't that what you were making yesterday?"

"I-I-I wanted to keep it a secret from Mr Snickletinkle," she stammered. "I thought it might come in useful."

"What does it do?" Trixie asked.

Gloria didn't answer. Instead, she took a big swig of the red liquid and pushed the cork back into the top. She let out a little burp and then vanished. As you might expect, this caught Trixie and Colin by surprise and they both leapt to their feet to look for their friend.

"I'm still here." Gloria giggled, though she was nowhere to be seen. "I'm invisible. That's what the potion does. I'm sorry, Trixie. I got the idea from Esme after your Snaffleball match. It doesn't work for long, but hopefully for long enough." Now that they looked properly, Trixie and Colin could see that the bottle of potion was still visible and appeared to be floating in thin air.

Trixie and Colin took turns swigging from the bottle and soon enough all three were completely invisible.

"How do we know that we are still all together?" asked Colin. "I don't want to get lost on my own."

Gloria's voice made Colin jump as it came from just behind his ear. "I thought of that." Colin felt Gloria take his hand in hers and managed to take Trixie's in his other. "If we hold each other's hands, we should be fine."

Hand in hand, they set off back out of the library

and along the corridor to the teachers' tower. They were banking on Mr Hairsnit either being in his own office or talking to another teacher in theirs so that they could hear what he had to say. Halfway up the winding stairs that led to the offices, they passed by Miss Flopsbottom's office door. It was slightly ajar and they could hear Mr Hairsnit talking to the headmistress inside.

Trixie pulled the others back against the tower wall and pressed her ear as close as she dared to the gap in the door. She couldn't work out what the teacher was saying, but he was definitely angry about something and was giving Miss Flopsbottom some very stern orders.

Suddenly, the door flew open and Mr Hairsnit barged out of the headmistress's office. Trixie managed to duck back just in time otherwise he would have knocked her and her friends back down the steps. Quickly, Trixie pulled on Colin's arm and dragged her friends up the stairs as close to Mr Hairsnit as she dared. She felt sure that he would hear them breathing or the sound of their shoes on the steps, but he appeared to be so angry about whatever had happened in Miss Flopsbottom's office that he paid them no attention.

When at last they reached the floor that was home to Mr Hairsnit's office, Trixie held her breath and raced forwards until she was only a few inches behind the werewolf. This close she could see the short grey hairs on his head and neck and it suddenly struck her where the grey fur in the grate had come from. She didn't have time to tell the others. That would have to wait. For now, she needed to stay as close as possible to their teacher. When he opened the door to his office, Trixie made sure that they were close enough to follow him through before it swung shut.

The office could only be described as a tip. There were unmarked pieces of work scattered all over the desk and floor and piles and piles of books stacked in every corner and on every flat surface that wasn't already covered in paper. Trixie looked at them closely and realised that they were all books about Ancient Egyptian gods and their magic. No doubt he was trying to find out more about the Ankhstone, possibly even to find out the magic words that would allow him to use it.

Mr Hairsnit didn't bother to sit down. He was clearly very angry about something and started throwing papers and books around his office as he searched for something. Exasperated, he yanked open one of the drawers in his wooden desk and gathered something up his hands. He shoved it quickly into a pocket in his robe before Trixie had a chance to see what it was and raced back out of his office as noisily as he entered it.

"What was that all about?" asked Colin as soon as they were sure that the teacher wasn't coming back.

"I've no idea." Trixie was definitely curious about something and made her way over to the desk. "But whatever it was that he took, he left behind this wooden stand."

"I know what that is!" Gloria exclaimed as she dragged one of the heavy books from the top of a teetering pile and slammed it down in front of Trixie. "Look here." She pointed at a drawing of a solid gold cross with a looped top and a brilliant blue gemstone set in the middle. It was being placed by a beautiful Egyptian queen onto a wooden stand just like the one that Trixie was holding.

"So that was the stand that the Ankhstone was mounted on?" asked Colin who was still feeling the effects of his late night of mixing potions.

"I think it's very clear who stole the Ankhstone from the library. I can't believe he would do something like this." Gloria sounded upset that her hero had let her down.

"We have to tell Miss Flopsbottom before he uses it," urged Trixie. "Just imagine what might happen if he finds the words he needs to control it. He could have us all under his spell!"

"If he knew the queen when she was alive, he might already know the words," Gloria warned. "We've got to find Miss Flopsbottom, and it's got to be now."

As they trio looked down, Gloria's potion started to wear off and within seconds they were fully visible again. They ducked out of the office and raced back down the steps towards Miss Flopsbottom's before anybody could see them.

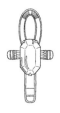

CHAPTER 8

The Truth

They didn't bother to knock when they finally reached Miss Flopsbottom's office. Instead, they burst straight into the room. Immediately, Trixie noticed that the headmistress still wasn't looking quite herself. She still wasn't blinking and her eyes were wide open.

"What on Earth is this all about?" Miss Flopsbottom demanded to know. "Why are you stampeding into my office unannounced?"

"Miss Flopsbottom."

They all tried to speak at once before Gloria took control. "Miss Flopsbottom, we have found out who stole the Ankhstone."

"I very much expect that you have. Especially

seeing as it was you." Miss Flopsbottom pointed a chubby finger at Trixie.

"Me?" Trixie was shocked. There is nothing worse than being accused of something that you know very well that you haven't done, and Trixie was determined to make that clear. "I haven't stolen anything at all, Miss Flopsbottom. You know that I haven't."

"I know very well that you have, my dear. Mr Hairsnit has been good enough to inform me of this not ten minutes ago. He wants you to be expelled. He got quite angry when I said I thought you deserved a fair trial, quite angry indeed. He made a very good argument, of course. I really do have no choice but to expel you."

"But she didn't steal it!" Colin was standing up and shouting. "It was Mr Hairsnit who stole it. He has the stand in his office."

"And his fur was on the grate next to the case in the library!" Trixie felt like she was fighting for her future at Monstacademy. "It really was him!"

"A very likely story indeed." Miss Flopsbottom

marched to the front of her desk and grabbed Trixie by her shoulders. "I am sure that he was just keeping the stand as evidence and that fur could have come from anywhere. I am going to take you to Miss Brimstone. She will deal with this. I have better things to be doing." With that, the head teacher marched Trixie out of her office and down a further flight of stairs. Colin and Gloria were left behind.

At the bottom of the stairs, Miss Flopsbottom knocked loudly on an old wooden door which was opened quickly by Miss Brimstone. Trixie's heart sank. It was well known that Miss Brimstone didn't care for Trixie and had never forgiven her for embarrassing Monstacademy at the Halloween Parade. She looked less than pleased at being disturbed, and her nose wrinkled even further when she saw that it was Trixie Grimble who was doing the disturbing.

It didn't take Miss Flopsbottom long to explain the situation to a sour-faced Miss Brimstone. When she had finally finished, Miss Brimstone ushered Trixie into her office. This office was quite the opposite to Mr Hairsnit's and not a paper was crinkled or ruffled. Everything was lined up neatly and even the pens and pencils seemed to know their place.

"I promise it wasn't me—" Trixie started before Miss Brimstone waved her into silence.

"I am quite sure that it wasn't." Trixie breathed a sigh of relief. "I am quite sure that you are not clever enough to steal the Ankhstone." Trixie hung her head and her cheeks went red. "However, Miss Flopsbottom seems quite convinced that it was you. She is not usually wrong, is she?"

"I don't know," Trixie wailed.

"Though even I must admit, she has been acting a little…strange lately. Think, girl. Who was she talking to right before she suspected you?"

Trixie remembered the argument with Mr Hairsnit that she had heard through the crack in the door. "Mr Hairsnit. He was using the Ankhstone to control Miss Flopsbottom?"

"Well done, Trixie. Perhaps you are not so dim

after all!" Trixie didn't like the accusation but said nothing. She was just happy that Miss Brimstone seemed to believe her. "So it would seem that our dear headmistress is being controlled by Mr Hairsnit. I have long suspected Mr Hairsnit of being up to no good, but I never suspected he would do something so evil as this. At least it seems we will finally be able to prove it."

"How can we stop him from controlling Miss Flopsbottom?" Trixie didn't like the idea of a grumpy Miss Flopsbottom for the rest of her time at Monstacademy. Miss Brimstone was grumpy enough on her own.

"For that, we need a queen. For now, though, it's off to lessons with you. Don't you have Snaffleball training?"

"I should, but my uniform has gone missing. It disappeared out of my wardrobe whilst I was in lessons the other day. I completely forgot about it until now. I'd only just found one that fit."

"Curious indeed. Have you possibly misplaced it?"

"No! I promise, I put it back carefully. It's just gone."

"Well, I'll send a message to Mr Fetch to make sure you are given a new uniform right away. We can't have you playing in just your vest again, now can we?" Miss Brimstone chuckled to herself as she scribbled a note on a scrap of paper and handed it to Trixie. "Off you go now. Tomorrow, we have a thief to catch."

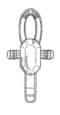

CHAPTER 9

Face the Music

In fact, it took the best part of three days for Miss Brimstone to get Queen Ankhesenamun to come back to the school. She had been on a Hawaiian cruise when the message had reached her, and so Monstacademy had sent Mr Snickletinkle to fetch her back. Even as a bat, he was exceptionally strong, and so he'd been able to fly her back in the dead of night without being spotted by too many people.

Being seen wasn't really a problem for them, after all, who'd believe you if you said that you'd seen a bat flying along holding an Ancient Egyptian queen wearing a grass skirt and drinking out of a coconut?

Once she arrived, Miss Brimstone and Trixie took her straight to Miss Brimstone's office where they sat her down and carefully told her everything that had happened including the bizarre behaviour of the headmistress.

"Oh, I am so embarrassed!" Queen Ankhesenamun wailed. "How did I not recognise him? He was one of our dearest friends at the time. Before the incident anyway."

"Incident? What incident?" Trixie asked. There

had been no mention of anything like that in the books.

"Well, we always suspected that Heka-Messes was jealous of our position as pharaoh and queen, but he was always very polite and courteous. Then one day, he snapped. He appeared to go quite mad. He started shouting about how the pyramids were out to get him, and he started wearing his robes as a cape and running around naked. Then, he decided that Bastet, the royal cat, was looking at him in a funny way and so he challenged it to a game of Senet, a little bit like your chess. What's worse is the cat won!"

"That sounds terrible." Trixie meant it as well. She couldn't imagine Mr Hairsnit in just a robe and nothing else.

"There really was only one thing for it. It was for his own good, of course."

"What did you do?" even Miss Brimstone was curious now.

"We threw him to the crocodiles. Terrible stuff really."

"I imagine that he held a bit of a grudge after that?" asked Trixie cautiously. Queen Ankhesenamun was clearly not a woman to be trifled with.

"It would certainly appear so. We thought he'd been eaten up, every last bone. I suppose it's harder for a werewolf to be eaten than a human. Come to think of it, we never did see those crocodiles again." Now it was Queen Ankhesenamun's turn to look uncomfortable.

"Did he know the words that he would need to say to make the Ankhstone work?" Miss Brimstone asked, cutting to the chase.

"I never told him them, but he may have heard me say them. I was never very good at remembering things either, so I had one of our slaves carve the words into my chamber walls so that I would always remember them. I suppose he may have read that."

Miss Brimstone scowled at the queen. Trixie knew that look well. It said "I do not enjoy dealing with buffoons, and you are a buffoon of the highest order." Miss Brimstone had used it on Trixie a lot.

"How do we stop him now? Will Miss Flopsbottom be under his spell forever?"

"No, we can fix this." The queen seemed happy that she might be able to help put everything back to normal. "All you need to do is read the same words to whoever controls the Ankhstone, and they will give it back. Anybody that they were controlling will get their own minds back. They'll also have a strange feeling that they are actually a watermelon for a while, but we've never been able to work out why."

"Lovely." Miss Brimstone was reaching the end of her tether. People thinking that they were watermelons and teachers wandering around with robes on their head was not something that she was cut out for. "And what are these magical words?"

"I'd rather not say." Queen Ankhesenamun looked sheepish.

"Without your help, we will never get the stone back," Trixie tried to persuade her. "This really is all your fault anyway."

"Fine." The queen gave in. "It is a spell. It's not very good and remember I didn't make it up. It was passed to me by my relatives." She coughed to clear her throat before launching into the poem.

The gods are powerful,
May they reign forever,
Do as I say,
Or be crocodile dinner!

The queen went red. "I told you it wasn't very good. Not a lot rhymes with 'forever'!" Miss Brimstone's face was as solid as rock. She looked as though she'd sucked on a lemon. Without saying a word, she took Trixie by the hand and led her from the room.

"That was unexpected." Trixie tried to lighten the mood. Miss Brimstone was clearly surrounded by dark clouds, and there was no clear patch on the horizon. Trixie gave up and allowed herself to be led up the stone steps towards Mr Hairsnit's office.

When they arrived, the door was half open and there was a loud sound of hurried packing coming from inside. Miss Brimstone didn't bother to knock which was lucky really because as she burst through the door Mr Hairsnit was halfway out of the window. The large, leather suitcase that he was dragging was clearly giving him some trouble.

"Oh no you don't!" Miss Brimstone picked up one of the heavy books from an unstable pile next to the door and threw it at Mr Hairsnit. Trixie was very impressed as the book flew straight across the cluttered office and struck the escaping teacher in the back of the head. He fell to the floor with a soft thump. "You are not the only one who used to be a Snaffler." Miss Brimstone winked at Trixie and dragged Mr Hairsnit over to his chair. He was groaning something about it not being fair and how the Ankhstone was rightfully his.

"Mr Hairsnit, please do be quiet. We don't care who the stone belongs to. All we care about is that you have used it to control people at Monstacademy. I really can't stand for that."

Mr Hairsnit's head was starting to clear, and he tried to stand up. Trixie hadn't realised just how strong Miss Brimstone was until that point. She held the snarling werewolf down with ease.

"Where is the Ankhstone?" she asked. Mr Hairsnit didn't reply, but Trixie had been watching his eyes. As soon as they flickered towards the desk drawer, she knew where it was.

"It's here, Miss Brimstone." She held the solid gold jewellery aloft. It was very heavy.

"Thank you." Miss Brimstone took the stone and looked at Mr Hairsnit with a glare angrier than any Trixie had seen before. As Trixie watched, Miss Brimstone recited the spell and something inside Mr Hairsnit vanished. He seemed to relax a little bit. "Now you will leave this country, and I never want to see you again. Is that clear?"

Mr Hairsnit didn't respond. He leapt to his feet and dragged his suitcase out of the door and left. After seeing Miss Brimstone's face, Trixie was sure that he would never dare to come back.

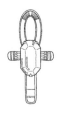

CHAPTER 10

Making Amends

Once they had taken the Ankhstone back from Mr Hairsnit, there was nothing much left to do. Their first job was to check that Miss Flopsbottom was back to her normal self. They found her sobbing quietly at her desk with a pile of books wedged behind her door. It took Trixie and Miss Brimstone a while to push the door open, but when they did they were relieved to see that Miss Flopsbottom looked much more like her old self. Her eyes weren't as wide anymore, and she was blinking again. She was also blowing her nose almost constantly on the white tissues that normally lived in her sleeve.

"I am so sorry for all of the trouble I've caused,"

she wailed as soon as they'd made her a strong cup of tea and explained everything that had happened.

"It's really not your fault, Miss Flopsbottom." Trixie tried her best to reassure the headmistress. "You were under the spell of an Ancient Egyptian god. It's not every day that happens!"

"But to think, I so nearly gave you some of that horrible potion that Heston brewed…I wanted to make you small so that I could flush you away down the toilet. Oh, the horror!"

Trixie glanced at Miss Brimstone who remained stony-faced.

"I didn't know that." Trixie managed. "But the important thing is that you didn't. I'm still here, and I'm perfectly fine."

The voluminous head teacher blew her nose loudly. It sounded like a cow trying to play the trumpet with its bottom.

"Was I the only one he controlled?"

"We think so. If he controlled you, the headmistress, he probably didn't think he needed to control anyone else. He didn't consider that our young trio might ignore your orders and do whatever they pleased anyway." Miss Brimstone was trying her hardest to be sympathetic to the large blubbering mess in front of her. It wasn't coming easily. This definitely fell under the category of what Miss Brimstone like to call silliness.

"Certainly, none of the children have been displaying any odd behaviour." Miss Brimstone looked across to Trixie. "At least no more so than normal. The staff are normally as mad as a box of angry pigeons anyway, so it's harder to tell."

"Well, there was one thing…" Trixie trailed off. She had an idea but didn't want to tell the teachers just yet. She might be wrong, after all. She made her excuses to leave. "I've just got to check something."

She darted out of the office and headed towards the girls' dormitories. She wasn't sure what to expect, but she had to find out. There had been one child who was acting oddly, even for them. Of course, it could just be perfectly normal. Normal for a school full of monsters anyway. On the other hand…

All of the girls' rooms were empty. It was dinnertime in the main hall, so they would all be eating. Nevertheless, there was a soft whimpering sound coming from the basement just below the rooms. Carefully and trying her best to be quiet, Trixie opened the door. There was a candle burning somewhere at the bottom of the stairs and it gave off a spooky, flickering glow.

Following the whimpers, Trixie edged down the stone steps and saw exactly what she had been hoping to find. Huddled against the wall and holding a single white candle was Esme Furfang. She looked up at Trixie with bright red eyes. She had obviously been crying for a long time.

"It's okay, Esme. I know you didn't mean it." Trixie sat down next to the werewolf and put her arm around her. "You were under a spell. I think Mr Hairsnit wanted me to stop investigating, and he thought that by embarrassing me during the Snaffleball match I would stop. He forgot that I'm always embarrassing myself so a little more didn't hurt!" she tried to lighten the mood, but Esme was feeling very glum indeed. "Was it you who stole my Snaffleball uniform as well?"

Esme nodded.

"Can I have it back?"

Another nod.

"What did you tell Miss Flopsbottom that I'd done to you?"

Esme looked sheepish. "Mr Hairsnit told me that you had stolen the Ankhstone and tried to hide in my room. My clothes and bedsheets were everywhere, and, you know, I was under his spell so I believed him and told Miss Flopsbottom. I don't think she'd have believed me if she wasn't under a spell herself. I'm sorry."

"Listen, I know you would never have done any of that stuff—"

Esme cut her off. "I wanted to, though. That's why I'm so upset. I've wanted to do that to you since you embarrassed me last term."

"But you wouldn't have done it unless you were under a spell, would you?"

"I guess."

"I really didn't mean to embarrass you last term. It really was an accident. I'm just *that* clumsy." Trixie was relieved to hear Esme let out a little chuckle. "I'd really love it if we could be friends. I seem to have enough enemies as it is."

Esme laughed properly this time and allowed Trixie to help her to her feet. Trixie helped her back up the steps to the tower and left her in her bedroom to get some sleep. Miss Flopsbottom had mentioned how she hadn't had any sleep at all since she'd been under Mr Hairsnit's control and that all she wanted to do now was to rest.

Besides, Trixie had one last job to do. She found Colin and Gloria sat in their usual corner in the main hall. That night would be a full moon, and so Colin was in full poodle mode. He was curled up in his basket chewing on his pink bone. He was fast asleep. The bone squeaked in time with his breathing. Gloria had decided to be more adventurous and was chewing on an apple for a change. Trixie sat down next to them with a big smile. When she had shaken Colin awake and was sure that she had their full attention, she told them the whole story. There were lots of gasps (and barks) and questions, but eventually she had caught them up.

"And so you and Esme are best friends, are you now?" Gloria asked. Trixie could sense a hint of jealousy in her voice.

"We're just going to stop being enemies, I think." Trixie laughed. "You'll always be my favourite vege*scarian*!"

"Woof?"

"What shall we do now?" Gloria translated. She could always understand Colin when he was in his *other* shape.

"We've got the rest of the term to get through," Trixie moaned. "Who knows what kind of trouble we'll get into before the summer holidays."

The three of them laughed out loud and finished their dinner. Not sure what lay in store for them, they went back to their bedrooms to get ready for bed. Trixie was right, they had a whole term of lessons left to get through. She couldn't believe how much had happened, and it was only the second week back after Christmas.

The first step for all of them though was to get some much needed sleep. That night, as Trixie lay her head down on her pillow, she smiled. No matter what happened, at least she'd have her friends around her.

As she started to fall to sleep, she tried very hard to forget the image of Mr Hairsnit playing chess with a cat in nothing more than his underwear.

Making Amends

Amazing Egyptian Facts

1 The Egyptians ruled their lands for nearly 3000 years starting in **3100BC**! That's longer than all of the time that has passed since Alexander the Great defeated them in **332BC**!

2 Queen **Ankhesenamun** actually was the wife of **King Tut**. More than that, she was also his half-sister! Weird!

3 **Heka** was the Ancient Egyptian god of magic and medicine. Does that make **Mr Hairsnit** the son of a god?

4 Only the richest Egyptians could afford to be mummified when they died. To make a mummy, you first had to remove all the gooey bits. The **stomach**, **intestines**, **lungs** and **liver** were all placed in containers called **canopic jars**. The **brain** was pulled out through the nose in tiny little pieces (eugh!) but the heart was left inside the body to be weighed by the god **Anubis**.

5 There were roughly **170** different **Pharaohs** of Ancient Egypt. Imagine having to learn all of their names in history class!

Number Puzzles!

Can you solve these number puzzles? Each symbol can only appear once in each row and column.

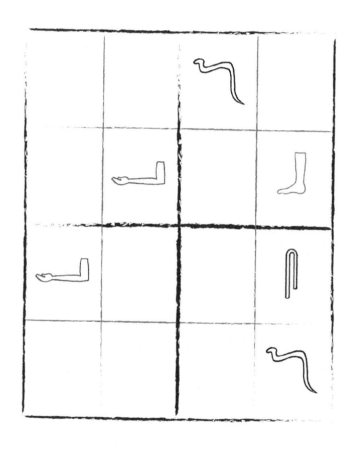

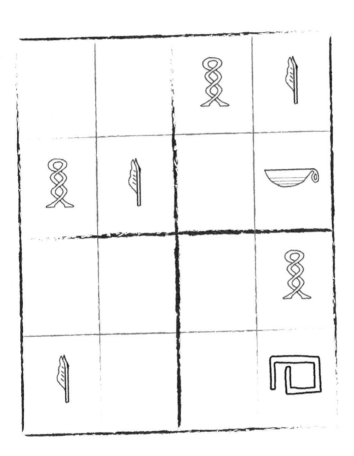

Word Spiral

```
A G R   E N O T S H K N A L F
T U T   A N U G T S A M N L F
H P Y   D S P H E K H E K A L
A Y M   S N Y           H B T
N R M   E A R   M I D   E E I
R A U   N F A   K E S   S L N
S M M   A N U B I S E   E F S
N I K   B A L L H T B   N F R
I D E   N U B S I E R   A A I
T S T               M N A
S E N E T B Y R Q X A O U S H
T P T U T A N K H A M E N U Y
T U K P Y R A N E B H K A M E
```

Ankhesenamun   Mummy
Anubis   Pyramid
Ankhstone   Senet
Hairsnit   Snaffleball
Heka   Tutankhamen

Monstacademy leaps from the page and into your ears in the exciting series of audiobooks, narrated by Ruth Bailes.

Search **Audible** for **Monstacademy,** and hear Trixie's adventures brought to life.

Stay in touch!

Sign up for my newsletter at
http://mattbeighton.co.uk
and get **exlusive information** about Monstacademy, writing tips and tricks and learn about whatever else I'm working on!

Want to read more?

Use the code **SUPERFAN** to get **10% off*** any books at

http://mattbeighton.co.uk

Slimy secrets and a sneaky traitor!

The most treacherous Monstacademy Mystery yet!

There's a traitor at Monstacademy!

When the most important monster in the country pays Monstacademy a visit, the threat of their school closing hangs over Trixie and her friends like a black cloud. To make matters even worse, there's a traitor in the ranks.

Who is making things go wrong at just the right time? It's a mystery that Trixie and Colin will have to solve on their own, unless they can convince Gloria to help them save the day once again.

Will a surprise visit from the Grand High Monster spell the end for Monstacademy?

Available now!

The mountains are full of dark secrets...

Trixie, Gloria and Colin are off on a trip to Peru to study ancient monsters. When they arrive and find that the children of the local school for monsters are disappearing, it becomes a race against time. Has a dark secret that's been trapped in the mountains come back to haunt them all? Has an ancient Inca curse been released? Or is it somebody much closer to home?

The Machu Picchu Mystery is the spookiest Monstacademy mystery yet.

With Trixie and her friends on the case, whatever evil is at large has a fight on its hands!

Can they find the missing monsters and solve the Machu Picchu Mystery? There's only one way to find out...

Available now!

About The Author

Matt Beighton is a full-time writer, born somewhere in the Midlands in England during the heady days of the 1980s. He is happily married with two young daughters who keep him very busy and suffer through the endless early drafts of his stories.

Matt's books have been read around the world and awarded the LoveReading4Kids "Indie Books We Love" and Readers' Favorite 5 Star Awards.

Having spent many years as a primary-school teacher, Matt Beighton knows how to bring stories to life. He regularly visits schools and runs creative workshops that ignite a passion for words.

If you have enjoyed reading this book, please leave a review online. Your words really do keep me going!

To find out more visit
www.mattbeighton.co.uk

Printed in Great Britain
by Amazon

87370343R10068